The Chilly Little Penguin

Russell Punter

Illustrated by Stephen Gulbis

Reading Consultant: Alison Kelly
Roehampton University

Once, there was a little
penguin called Perry.

Perry and his family
lived at the South Pole.

It was always
very cold.

One day, Perry found
a box.

He saw something
yummy inside.

But he was too cold
to eat it.

Perry went to see his grandpa.

"I need to get warm, Grandpa," he said.

"Try skating," said Grandpa. "That will warm you up."

Okay.

Perry went to the
frozen lake.

He skated up and down...

...and round and round.

He skated all morning.

"Are you warm, now?"

"N...no," said Perry.

Perry went to see his grandma.

"I need to get warm, Grandma," he said.

13

"Try swimming," said Grandma. "That will warm you up."

Okay.

Perry dived into
the water.

Splash!

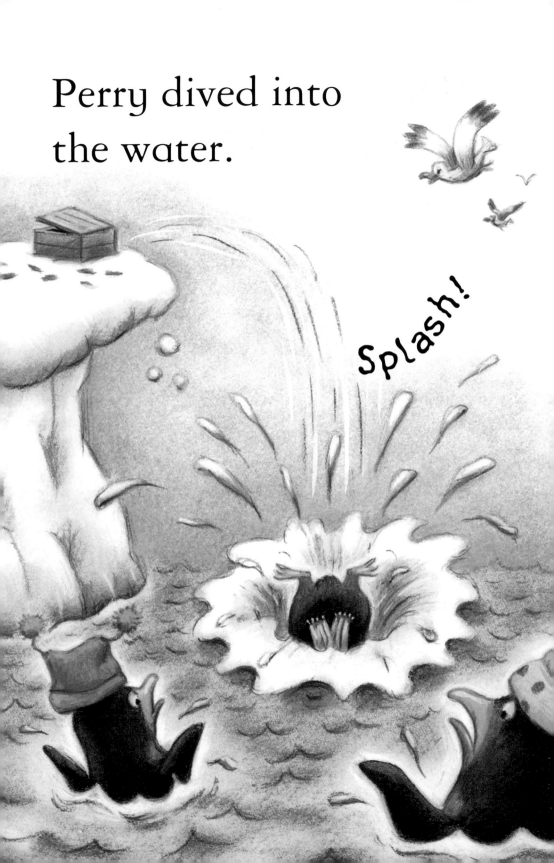

He swam up and down...

...and round and round.

He swam all afternoon.

"Are you warm, now?"

"N...no," said Perry.

Perry went to see his
sister, Pippi.

"I need to get warm,
Pippi," he said.

"Try sliding down the hill," said Pippi. "That will warm you up."

Okay.

Perry went to the top
of the hill.

...and round and round.

He slid around all
evening.

"Are you warm now?"
everyone asked.

"Yes, I'm boiling,"
said Perry.

He opened the box.

"Now I can enjoy this ice cream," he said.

25

PUZZLES

Puzzle 1

Can you spot the differences between these two pictures? There are six to find.

Puzzle 2
Find these things in
the picture:

beak   box   scarf

glasses   hat

Puzzle 3
Find the opposites.

old

dry

cold

young

wet

hot

Answers to puzzles

Puzzle 1

Puzzle 2

hat

glasses

beak

box

scarf

Puzzle 3

old

young

cold

hot

wet

dry

Series editor:
Lesley Sims

This edition first published in 2017 by Usborne Publishing Ltd.,
Usborne House, 83-85 Saffron Hill, London EC1N 8RT, England.
www.usborne.com Copyright © 2017, 2008 Usborne Publishing Ltd.